FROM PARIS
with love

A HOLIDAY SHORT

C. Wilson

From Paris with love
Copyright© 2022
C. WILSON

<u>Follow C. Wilson on social media</u>

Instagram: @authorcwilson
Facebook: @CelesteWilson
Join my reading group on Facebook:
Cecret Discussionz
Follow my reading group on Instagram:
@CecretDiscussionz
Twitter: @Authorcwilson_

Tell me what you think of this story in a customer review.
Thank you,
-xoxo-
C. Wilson

LETTER TO MY READERS

This book is STRICTLY for the readers that have ridden the Bleek and Eternity rollercoaster. This one is for the readers that have read *A Love Affair for Eternity 1-4* AND the last holiday spin-off *Love in-between Eternity's Holiday.* If you haven't...
I'm going to need you to CLEAR THE AREA. Go back and read those and then come back to read this heat.
This special SHORT treat is for my Cecret Discussionerz...
I love y'all

-xoxo-
C. Wilson

Chapter 1

Bleek sat in the center of the suede sectional sofa that stood on top of a massive white colored plush rug. He watched as the fire danced in the fireplace. The Christmas carols lightly played in the background. Although the house was still the melody echoed throughout the massive walls of his kingdom. He reached for the cup that was placed on the glass coffee table just in front of him. Lightly he moved his hand in a circular motion to mix in the melting ice cubes with the cognac.

Peace had finally found his front door yet he was troubled. Something was bothering him and he knew exactly just what it was.

"I woke up looking for you."

The soft angelic sound of Eternity, his wife, caused him to look over his shoulder. She wore a sheer robe with nothing underneath. A risky move she could get away with because their nine-year-old and four-year-old daughters were fast asleep in their beds.

Eternity rounded the sofa and then straddled him. She took the glass from his hand and then placed it on the coffee table before wrapping her arms around his neck.

"What's up with you?" she asked.

Gently he kissed her neck.

"Nothing."

"Malik Browne... I know when ya ass gets to lying. You tossed and turned all night before leaving the bed. Something is bothering you."
So connected with one another she felt his energy in her own sleep. He threw his head back and then sighed deeply. There was no way that he would spoil the mood by telling his wife that a woman from his past was possibly walking around with a ten-year-old child of his.

"Ma, it's work."
Eternity lived in the comfort that he had created for her so she dropped the issue. If Bleek said it was work, then it was work.

Years of drama taught Eternity that if the problem isn't evident then don't go searching for it.

"Okay."
She tapped his lips before getting up from his lap.

"Uh uh, bring it back," he grabbed her hand and then sat her back down on his lap, "you can't come out the room looking like this and then think ya ass gone leave without at least sitting on it."
She smirked before pulling down his pajama pants just enough to release his brick lumber.

Around the house, he never wore a shirt. His tatted chest was artwork to her. A comfy canvas that she had the pleasure of consistently sleeping on for the past ten years. She kissed him deeply as she lifted her body slightly to ease down on his rod.

6

"Sssss..." he hissed once he felt her warm, gushy insides.

She worked her hips in a circular motion. He leaned up, grabbed his cup from the table, and then drank the remainder of his drink before placing the glass on the couch.

"You lost ya mind putting that shit on my sofa?"

"Did you lose your mind starting with me tonight," he growled into her ear as he grabbed her hips firmly before thrusting her from underneath.

"Malikkkk..."

"Uh uh, don't cry now take this shit. You wanted to start right."

Eternity threw her head back as her nails dug into the back of the couch. Her claws left indentations in the suede material.

"I love you..." she moaned out as her sweet nectar coated his shaft.

Right behind her, he finished. A quickie, while the kids were sleeping, was their go-to. They had the nights of endless lovemaking already. That's what got them the kids, to begin with.

Bleek kissed from her neck up to her face as he spilled seeds inside of her. They didn't plan on more children but he didn't mind a village from her. Eternity was perfect in every way to him. She made a nigga want to put a custom tracker in her cervix. So when given the opportunity, he never passed up on it. In his mind, God kept gifting them with girls because there was no replacement for the son that they shared almost eleven years ago that had passed away. There was no redoing his junior. As soon as she stood up and made her exit to go and clean herself, his mind went right back to being troubled. He had no idea how he was going to tell his wife that he was the father of a ten-year-old boy.

"Damn," he mumbled as he pulled his pajama pants and underwear back to his waist, grab the glass that was on the couch, and then headed to the kitchen.

✳✳✳

"Come on pick it up MJ! Pick it up!"

Paris locked her phone and then placed it in her lap as she watched the coach scream at her son. Basketball was his sport and he was damn good at it. At ten years old he hit three-point shots like Kobe. Effortlessly, Spaulding flew out his little hands and into the air hitting buckets every time. He carried his team as a shooting guard. She watched his legs pick up as he ran laps with his teammates.

"Ms. Shaw, you know you don't have to stay for the entire practice right?"

Paris smiled lightly at the coach she knew had a crush on her.

"I barely get to make any of his games the least I can do is sit in on practice."

Following in her father's, the prior Florida state attorney general, footsteps Paris had become a Criminal Justice lawyer. Being a single mom and having her career was a hard task but she made it work. She flipped her phone over and looked at the face when it vibrated in her lap.

Get the brakes done and get the car an oil change...

Little reminders she put into her calendar because she was always on the move.

MB Autos had been handling the maintenance on her cars for over ten years. It was so bittersweet having the business still service her vehicle after the romantic relationship had ended with the owner of the multi-chain mechanic shop.

Swish

"Good shot MJ."

Paris looked up from her phone and saw that her son was standing at the free-throw line with his tongue resting on the side of his mouth. *It's shit like that,* Paris thought to herself. Little mannerisms that her son had reminded her so much of his father.

Swish.

When his second shot made it in she clapped her hands. The team was getting ready for their last game before Christmas. It was rare that his little league had games that ran this close to the holidays but they had been having such a successful year that a championship game was necessary.

"Alright, y'all we gone play three mock games and call it a day okay?"

"Okay coach," the boys said in unison. While her boy played Paris engaged back in her phone. She hovered over the name *Malik*. So many memories of her past love flooded her. *Gone too soon.* She thought as she shook her head from left to right to put the tears on standby.

To the world, Malik Browne was nothing more than a ghost. A staged plane crash he had to partake in almost ten years prior made the world believe that he and Eternity were dead. The only ones that knew he was still breathing and in the flesh were his immediate family. Paris thought that she could do this parenting shit on her own but as MJ got older he began to become rebellious.

The only thing that kept him in line was his love for basketball. He was becoming such a headache, but he was her headache and she wouldn't trade him for anything in the world.

Paris stared at the waxed gymnasium floor as she thought about the day that could have changed her life drastically...

"Are you ready Paris?" the nurse asked.

Paris stared down at the hospital socks that graced her feet. Her natural pigeon-toe stance had her two big toes touching. Her stomach was growling and that's because she couldn't consume anything since midnight. She was about to make God's choice. Getting rid of life, the life inside of her stomach. She and Bleek ended on horrible terms but why did she have to get rid of her child because of it?

Originally the idea was hers but that was out of anger, that was her wanting to get him back out of spite. Once the word "abortion" left her lips and she saw that he agreed so much so that he made sure to send her with supervision, she was heartbroken.

"Paris?" The nurse tried getting her attention again but it wasn't working.
Paris was cold and numb, not only because the temperature was very frigid in the clinic but because her emotions were sea-sawing on what she should do.

"The escort that's waiting on me is making me get this abortion. I don't want to, I want to keep my baby."
She broke down in tears.

"Has she ever physically abused you?"

"No just mental tactics," Paris was laying it on thick to get the woman to feel sympathetic for her.

"Okay... well come with me we will have to alert the authorities."

"No please," Paris grabbed the woman's arm and pleaded with her, "I just need her to believe that I got the abortion."

"Okay..." the woman twisted her mouth like she was deep in thought.

Paris knew that she was asking a lot of the woman. She was asking her to basically put her job on the line.

"Come with me. We can handle this." The woman stared into Paris' round brown orbs and knew that she had to help her. Her situation was too close to home.

"I'm gonna handle this for you." She reassured Paris again while leading the way to an examination room in the back...

"Ma... Ma come on now. You all lost in the sauce let's go, practice over."

Paris blinked her eyes repeatedly before focusing her sights on her pride and joy. His thick eyebrows were scrunched together with much attitude. He was the spitting image of his father. His stance and his looks.

"Ma let's roll... dag." MJ picked his backpack off the floor and then tossed it onto his back. Paris sucked her teeth as she followed her son out. *Even his damn attitude is like his father,* she thought as they entered the parking lot together.

"Aht aht the back seat little boy."

"Man... but Pop Pop lets me ride in the front when I ride with him."

"Well, I'm not your grandfather you gone ride in the back around these parts."

MJ huffed and puffed as he opened up the back door and then got in.

"Are you excited about your basketball game coming up?"

"Yeah, I'm geeked for sure Ma."

Paris looked in the rearview mirror and saw that her son was engaged in his cell phone. Most likely playing a basketball game. When she looked back to the road she saw a car quickly cut in front of her which caused her to stomp on her brakes.

Honk!

"Asshole!" She yelled as she put her middle finger up.

"You okay MJ?" She quickly looked to the back to see her son's eyebrows bunched in anger.

"Yeah I'm straight he's a jerk. Yeah, you ASSHOLE!"

"Malik Leon Browne!"

"Sorry Ma," he huffed as she got into the next lane and went around the driver who almost caused the accident.

He eyed the driver with a look that could have killed.

"What were we talking about?" Paris tried to get her mind off of the bullshit that almost occurred.

"My basketball game Ma. All the boy's dads are coming. It just sucks that I don't have a dad for me."

Paris tapped the steering wheel while in deep thought. She knew that eventually, MJ would ask for his father. It started about three years ago. She didn't know when was too young to explain death to her child but she had found a way to let him know that he was loved and being watched over.

A boy is always going to want and then eventually need their father. It broke her heart that she couldn't give him his.

"How about I see if Pop Pop can come to the game? Would you like that Stinky Pooh Putt?"

"Maaa come onnn with that nickname. You said that at one of my practices and now the boys be clowning me."

"Okay, I'm sorry big MJ."

"There we go..."

Paris smirked as she pulled into her parent's driveway.

"Aight kiddo here's your stop."

"Ma I can watch myself Pop Pop and Nana don't have to."

"Yeah right... see you later love you."

Paris tilted her head towards the back seat and he quickly kissed her on the cheek. He flung the back door open to make his exit.

"Aye... I said love you."

"Love you too."

"Love you most."

MJ turned around and gave his mom a smirk that melted her heart. *So much like your fucking father,* she thought as she watched him wave bye and then walk into his grandparent's house. She had a long list of things to do before the holidays and finding a family member of Malik's and getting in contact with them was one of them. She at least wanted her son to know someone that knew his father. At least someone could speak of all the good that Malik Browne had graced the world with.

Chapter 2

"Come on pussy make that shot" Sha was taunting Bleek.

Swish

"Ahhhh," Bleek stuck his tongue to the side while his hands were still in the air.

"Aight you got it G. You got it. You the goat."

Sha lifted his shirt and then rubbed his abdomen as he tried to catch his breath.

"It feels muthafucking good to be back in Florida."

Bleek looked in his best friend's direction and felt the need to mention his gains.

"Yeah, them croissants in Paris was your bestie, huh?"

"Huh, what?" Sha dropped his shirt and then laughed slightly, "nigga this is baby weight."

"Baby weight my ass, you just been lazy not working out with me."

"Yeah... yeah, we hooping now. Late as fuck at that. Now what you called me over for?" Sha began to walk to the nearby bleachers.

On Bleek's estate in Florida, he had a basketball court, a pool, a gun range and so much more. He was a firm believer in his home being his sanctuary so his land held everything that he needed. He followed behind Sha towards the bleachers. After picking up his phone, he opened up his Instagram app and then showed Sha what had caught his eye the day before.

"Damn this little nigga can hoop. The back of that jersey says, Browne. Let me find out nigga, God created a little you? That's dope man. You should donate to that boy school—"
The audio from the video cut Sha off.

"Although he's ten years old he had a lot to say about this upcoming holiday game. So Malik Browne—"
"Dude it's MJ the people call me MJ"

"Fuck is this bro?" Sha asked with his brow dented.
"The fucking end to my marriage Sha that's what the fuck that is."
Sha brought the phone closer to his eyes, "damn this lil muthafucka look just like you."

Bleek plopped down on the empty space beside Sha. With his elbows pressing into his toned thighs he held the weight of his head within the palm of his hands.
"Damn bro..." Sha slid the phone in Bleek's direction, "how the fuck did you even come across this?"
"You know with the YMCA that me and Eternity own back in Brooklyn that I search local basketball teams and donate. I came across this

17

shit and man... I need to have a sit down with Paris this shit is crazy."

Sha stared off into space before he offered a response. To him, it was crazy how life worked. When his boy had finally found his happy ending the biggest bomb was about to be dropped on his doorstep.

"Doesn't she think that you're dead?"

"Yeah... shit the only people that know we aren't are you, Tori, Ty, and his family. Damn, I can't believe she would do this shit!"

"Do what shit bro? It takes two to tangle." Bleek cut his eye at Sha. He didn't want to hear the bullshit that he was currently on.

"I literally organized the whole abortion and even sent her with someone. Like how is this happening?"

"It's you giving the bitch an option to get an abortion. A nigga like me woulda kicked her ass right on down some stairs. I'm talking bottom of black Air Force Ones to the bitch's spine."

Bleek laughed loudly. He needed the change in mood that Sha was offering. After he got his laughter out they both just sat in silence.

"So what you gone do?" Sha asked.

"I think I wanna go to his game."

Sha's nose crinkled with his screwed expression.

"You wanna do what now?"

"I just gotta see the little nigga up close and personal."

"I don't know bro. I think step one would be to get at his moms. Fuck you think she gone do when she see you at lil man's game."

Bleek's mental knobs were turning. He hadn't thought that far ahead. The only thing on his mind was the replica of himself that he watched repeatedly on his phone. He needed to see that chocolate flesh in person. He sat quietly as he thought about if he and Eternity's son if given the chance to grow older, would he have resembled him in such an uncanny way that Paris' son had.

He just knew that Paris had to hate him her entire pregnancy to spit out his twin like that. Suddenly he was saddened because although all loyalty went to his wife he hated that a woman, any woman, whether he hated them or not would have to go through a pregnancy alone. With his daughters, he waited on Eternity hand and foot. It had nothing to do with the fact that she was his wife. He held her to the highest of standards because she carried a piece of him within her.

She birthed his DNA and for that, he would forever be grateful. Paris went through an entire pregnancy without that emotional support from the other parent and that made him feel like shit. When it came to his flesh and blood, Bleek showed up every fucking time. Without question, without hesitation, he would stand ten toes down for his. He would burn down cities for his and when the judgment day came he would take any charge on the chin. The simple fact that his son, who he believed to be his son, lived ten years on earth without him was troublesome.

"Yo boy, I'm out."

Bleek broke from his daze. He dapped Sha up.

"You gone roll with me to this game right?"

Sha threw his head back and sighed in frustration. All an act because he knew damn well that he was going to make the run with Bleek. Sha was always a day one, ride until the wheels fall off ass nigga and when the wheels fell off he was the steal a car and keep riding ass nigga.

"Yeah, bruh I got you. I can't believe ya ass is trynna start some shit before the holidays. Eternity's ass ain't bout to cook shit for Christmas and then Tori's ass ain't about to give me no pussy until Easter cause you dragging me in this."

"Easter sex?"

Sha's eyes lit up like he was recalling the best memory.

"Hell yeah, she dresses up like a bunny and shit. Hide eggs around the house andddd—"

"Aight bruh too much info. Y'all weird as fuck."

Bleek shook his head with a chuckle as he watched his boy exit the gym. He made a note in the calendar on his phone of the game.

***

"Mam? You need help?"

It had been a while since Paris had walked through the doors of MB Autos. So spoiled still her father took her vehicle to get serviced whenever it was needed.

"Um yes..."

Paris twisted her hands together nervously as she walked closer to the desk. Her heels clicked across the floors as she closed the distance between her and the front desk receptionist.

"I wanted to know if any family of Malik Browne runs this now? Or anyone close to him."

A saddened expression showed on the white man's face.

"No mam. After his passing, a lawyer showed up and let me know that I had full ownership of this location right here. I'm not sure what happened with his other locations."

"Thank you..."

Paris turned on her heels and made her exit. She was sure that the new owner couldn't do much to help her.

When she got into her car she noticed that her brake light had come on but she was on a mission. She needed somebody that could deliver answers to her. After all, she didn't even know exactly what had happened to Malik. There was never a funeral service she just knew that he was pronounced dead along with who the news called his long-term girlfriend. Paris sucked her teeth just at the thought of how he had left her for another woman. The other woman, who she always knew was the better woman for him.

Before even dealing with Malik she knew that his heart was somewhere else and always had been. She drove through Coral Gables until her vehicle placed her outside of the gate of his estate. In the distance, she could see two white men exiting a vehicle and then walking up the five stairs that led to what used to be Malik's front door.

"New owners," she mumbled before pulling off. She tapped the steering wheel vigorously as she tried to think of her next move. With MJ's game approaching, she had to gather him some items for that. The quest to find someone connected to his father would have to wait.

Chapter 3

Eternity smiled when the bell to the front door went off. Moving back into Bleek's estate was a headache but she was ready to finally make it her own. Todd and Chaz were a married couple that specialized in interior design.

"Hello hunnies," Eternity said excitedly as she pulled the door open.

"Oh love it's been forever," Chaz ran his hand through his blonde hair before pulling her into a hug.

After faking their death, Eternity had reached out to the power couple to decorate her and Bleek's townhome in Paris. She pushed the door open so that both men could walk through.

"So where will we be setting up?"

Eternity led the way to one of the sitting areas. The couple placed their binders down and started pulling out pattern samples.

"So for the master how do you feel about a silver and bling."

"Malik is not going for all that diva shit, Chaz."

"Damn sure not. Don't get too cute with it."

Eternity looked up from the patterns and smiled when her man entered the room. His scent made it to her before he did.

"You're dressed dressed, where to?"

23

She overlooked his attire. His normal uniform of a sweatsuit was nowhere to be found. She dreaded when he tossed on a Nike Tech anyway. In her mind, every woman had a clear sight of that thick rod that she took ownership of when he wore those. So, seeing him in denim was satisfying.

That New York swag wasn't going anywhere. Butter Timberland boots graced his feet along with some distressed jeans paired with an off-white sweater. His low haircut had his silky textured hair rippled with waves.

"Hello hubbyyyy," Todd said with a smile.

"Cut that shit out," Bleek raised his eyebrow in Todd's direction before completely closing in the space between him and Eternity.

"Gotta make a quick move Ma," he gently kissed the side of her neck.

"Be careful."

She puckered up her lips and he gently kissed them.

"Always," he whispered before kissing her lips again.

The sound of feet running above their heads could be heard.

"Stop fucking running!" Eternity yelled at the top of her lungs.

Boom! Boom!

"Girls!"

The bass in Bleek's voice halted the movement above their head. The bangs and booms were replaced with silence. Eternity ran the house but Bleek was the force that made shit move.

"Daddy run the house, huh?" Chaz giggled.

Bleek smirked at Eternity before kissing her forehead. Her eyebrows were crinkled with anger.

"This why we're done with kids for real them girls don't muthafucking listen."

"They do listen. Just to me," Bleek laughed lightly before grabbing a handful of her behind, pulling her in close, and then kissing her one last time.

"See you in a bit."

"Yeah yeah," Eternity finished flipping through the pattern samples that were now scattered all across the table.

✱✱✱

"You sure shorty even still lives here?"

"Why wouldn't she? She owns the muthafucka."

"It's been years bro."

Bleek and Sha sat outside of Paris' house in a tinted white Trackhawk Jeep. A white Lexus drove around them and then pulled into the driveway. The driver of the vehicle sat in the car for a while.

"That's her?" Sha asked as both he and Bleek stared at the vehicle.

"Gotta be."

"You think your boy in there?"

"Shit I don't know."

"How you gone handle this bro?"

"Shit... I DON'T KNOW."

Bleek took his tatted hand and then wiped from his nose down to his beard. He stroked the facial hair that held specs of gray and then sighed before putting his hand into a fist and placing it on the steering wheel. *Renmen*, he stared at his son's name that graced the outside of his hand. Having a son, losing him, and then finding out years later that he had another one was eating him up inside.

When the door to the white Lexus swung open Bleek saw the heel of the Christian Louboutin hit the pavement first. Paris was sporting a pants suit. She reached into her car and grabbed her briefcase and coat before placing them over her forearm. The back door to the car opened and there he was. MJ tossed his backpack onto his back and then slammed the door shut before running to his mother's side. He grabbed the briefcase from her and her coat before running to the front door.

"Little nigga got manners and shit."

Sha nudged Bleek with his elbow as they both watched.

Paris opened the door for her and MJ and then just turned around and stared at the truck before she went inside and closed the door behind her. Bleek's windshield was tinted like the rest of the truck so he knew that she couldn't see him. He fumed silently because her guard was not up. What happened if he were a threat? She carelessly exited the vehicle and put her son, their son into harm's way. She didn't know who was in the vehicle and he hated how she moved. She was never the street-smart kind of chick. She didn't have to be.

In the beginning of their dating, he admired that about her. It was the different ambiance she possessed that drew him to her but in the end, he started to hate that about her.

"What we doing bro?"

"I just wanna sit for a minute."

Bleek was still trying to wrap his head around him fathering the child. For about an hour they sat outside of the residence and watched as lights turned on in one room and then off in others. Paris and MJ had to be turning down for the night. Especially with MJ's big game being the next day, Bleek knew that he better act fast before they called it a night.

When the light to the truck came on and Sha felt the breeze of air enter their space he looked to his left.

"Where you going?"

Bleek didn't answer Sha he just closed the driver's door behind him and then began walking up Paris' driveway towards her front door. When he got to the front door so many memories flashed through his mind. He used to have a key to this same house. He used to walk into this house effortlessly, freely, she let him do whatever he wanted to her in this house.

He peeked through the glass window of the door and saw the stairs to her home. Uncountable times he entered her body right there on those stairs. He sighed deeply before pressing the bell to the door. He stepped back to give space between himself and whoever was going to open the door. He stood there for a while and when he went to press the button again the door flew open.

"Sorry I took so long just keep the chang—"

When Paris' eyes met with Bleek's her words caught in her throat.

Standing in front of him she wore a nightgown with a plush robe over it. Her go to when they were together. Plenty of nights he hiked those moomoos up and went to town on her thick frame.

"This isn't possible."

Her hands covered her mouth as her head shook from left to right in disbelief.

"You don't say who when somebody rings your bell? You just swing the shit open?" Quickly the disbelief wore off and Paris placed one hand on her hip as much attitude was preparing to spew from her body.

"What gives you the fucking right to ring my muthafucking bell anyway?"

"Ma... you good?" Bleek looked behind her and could see the miniature version of himself standing at the top of the stairs.

"I'm fine boo go finish watching your play tapes." Paris pulled the door closed behind her as she closed the robe she wore over the nightgown.

"What the fuck are you doing here *dead man?*" She growled through clenched teeth.

"Is he mine?"

He had found himself in this situation twice in his life and he hated it. What he hated more than the situation he was in was the time it took for her to respond.

"Is he mine!?" This time bass filled his voice.

"Lower your fucking tone before you disturb this peacefulness I created for our son. ME," she slapped her own chest with the palm of her hand, "I created this for him on my fucking own. With no help from you!"

"I didn't know."

"And I didn't know you were alive. What was that a fucking hoax?"

29

Bleek looked away from her because he couldn't and didn't want to offer her an answer. What was done, was done and he was trying to move forward.

"Can I meet him?"

"Why did you fake your death?" she angrily clapped her hands in between each word, "What are you currently stealing someone's identity? That's illegal. You can put under the jail."

This was the shit that he hated about her. She was always by the book and technicalities. The type to walk the straight-and-narrow.

"I found my way around that and I had to, to protect my family."

Paris shook her head from left to right in disbelief.

She never quite understood just how much pull the man standing in front of her had. She knew Malik, the auto shop-owning gentleman. She had no idea who Bleek, the ruthless kingpin was.

"He is your family too Malik."

"I thought you were getting an abortion."

"At your request," she huffed.

His eyebrows bent in anger.

"YOU brought that shit up first don't go there."

When the sound of a car pulling into the driveway could be heard Bleek quickly turned around. He relaxed when he saw that it was a

Pizza Hut delivery car. The delivery driver walked up with two boxes and a smile. Paris went into the pocket of her robe to hand the man the money but Bleek went into his pocket to grab his wallet. After giving the man a fifty-dollar bill he told him to keep the change and sent him on his way. Bleek handed Paris the two boxes. She opened the front door.

"MJ come get this pizza and put it in the kitchen."

"Coming Ma."

The front door pulled open wider and Bleek looked on as the spit caught in his throat.

"Who this?"

"Boy take the boxes and go."

MJ looked Bleek up and down with a bushy brow. Bleek returned the same stare. The reflection was uncanny, the stance the same, and the brown orbs an exact match.

"Malik go."

Bleek looked Paris' way when he saw the young boy move to his government name. The name that his grandmother had given him, like Eternity, Paris gave to her son, their son. He waited until the young boy was out of sight to open his mouth.

"You named him after me."

"I did."

"Ughhh..." he groaned.

He turned around and stared at the truck he had just gotten out of.

"Can I come in?"

Paris looked skeptical. Their circumstances were horrible but she promised herself that before Christmas she would get in contact with her son's father's family and here she was doing something ten times better. She was giving her son his father in the flesh. She placed the loose hair in front of her face behind her ear.

"Um yeah, come on."

She opened the door just enough for Bleek to walk through. He closed the door behind himself and then locked it. As soon as he did his phone vibrated in his pocket.

Sha

"Yeah, bro?"

"What's going on you good?"

"Yeah, listen if you wanna dip off somewhere and spin back for me that's cool."

"Na my boy I'll be out here chilling these chairs recline back take ya time."

"Aight boy."

Bleek hung up the phone as he followed Paris to the kitchen. The décor in her home had changed drastically. She had always had a sense of design but the cream and earth tone colors of her home felt so welcoming.

"I would fuss about you still having those boots on but since this will be quick I'll let you slide."

When Bleek followed Paris into the kitchen he saw MJ sitting on a bar stool at the island counter engaged in his phone.

"You didn't eat yet Stinky Pooh Putt?"

"No I was waiting on you," he answered without looking up.

"Stinky Pooh Putt?" Bleek whispered, still loud enough for MJ to hear.

He locked his iPhone and then looked up at Bleek.

"Only my Ma calls me that. I wish she would stop. Who you?" he asked again with the same hostility he had in his voice when he had asked just moments ago.

Bleek had to chuckle because the boy had just as much fire in him as he did.

"MJ this is Malik... this is your dad."

The young boy tilted his head to the side and surveyed Bleek for a while. His eyes watered as he turned his glance to his mother.

"You said my dad was dead."

"Baby because that's what I thought. Had I known I swor—"

Bleek saw the disappointment on MJ's face and there was no way he was about to stand on the sidelines and watch Paris take all of the heat for his life decision.

"Your mom didn't know I was alive because I made it that way. I had to go away for a while to protect you, her, and the rest of my family."

Those little brown spheres that mirrored his turned in his direction. MJ quickly slid his body off of the bar stool and then ran full speed in Bleek's direction. Dropping down to his knees Bleek had his arms out as he took the young boy into his wings and then hugged him tightly. He was creasing the front of his boots and didn't give a fuck.

"Please don't be a lame dad. I hope you like Minecraft and Fortnite."
Bleek chuckled as he rubbed the boy's back.

"I'm the shit in Fortnite."

"Malik your language," Paris said as she watched on with watery eyes.

Her eyes fixated on the iced-out wedding band that graced his finger. She didn't know his relationship status and she had no want to know. All she wanted was a steady co-parent relationship. Her want to be with Malik had faded years ago, years before she ever knew of a hoax death. Towards the end of their dating, her feelings had slowly faded. The hugging duo broke their embrace and just stared one another in the eyes.

"You like pizza? Ma got pizza."

"Pizza cool."
MJ took the seat he just climbed out of and Bleek sat directly next to him. Paris opened one pizza box and then placed two slices onto two separate plates. She put one plate in front of Bleek and then another in front of MJ. She stood back as

she watched them eat. Both chewing the same exact way.

It was a shame to her how much they did alike although Malik wasn't given the chance to raise the boy. In between chewing the two engaged in conversation. Bleek was taking everything in. The boy's favorite color, his favorite game, everything. MJ dropped the crust of his pizza on his plate.

"I got a big game tomorrow."

"I know..." Bleek let slip out.

Both MJ and Paris looked at him.

"I'll be there."

"Really?" MJ asked with much excitement.

"Really...." Bleek confirmed.

"Really?" Paris asked with a raised eyebrow.

When Bleek looked up to give her his attention he saw that she was staring down at his hand. He twirled his wedding ring with his thumb before they made eye contact.

"Really..."

"Oooh, the boys gone be jealous 'cause my dad is dope. Like Ma look at these dope clothes. He got swag man."

Bleek laughed.

"What you be wearing little man?"

"Ma takes me to Hollister and—"

"Takes you where? Na tomorrow morning we gone go shop for you some new shit, aight?"

35

"Aight cool."

Bleek held his fist out and MJ gave him dap. Bleek cut eyes at Paris. She wore expensive threads so he didn't understand why she didn't practice the same for their child.

"Go and wash your hands and get in bed you got a big day tomorrow stink."

"Okay, Ma."

MJ stood from his seat and then started to make his exit.

"Dad?" He stood in the doorway of the kitchen.

Bleek looked up at him and tears started to come to his eyes. His heart was filled with so much joy because he was proud. Proud of the boy that was standing in front of him but saddened at the fact that he hadn't had the chance to raise him from the beginning.

"Thank you for not being dead."

Bleek stood from his seat and then closed the space between him and the boy. He hugged him and gently rubbed his back before placing a hand on his head and then rubbing it.

"Come on Dad you gone mess up the waves."

Bleek chuckled, "got a durag right?"

"Of course"

"Well brush and toss that on before bed. You spinning but you ain't fucking with me," Bleek said with a smirk.

"See you tomorrow," MJ called out as he climbed the stairs.

Bleek stood frozen in the doorway until the boy disappeared.

"Ms. Shaw," he resorted to what he used to call her, "you did good."

"I did, huh?" she said with a bright smile.

"Listen—" before he could even get the words out his phone vibrated in his pocket.

ALL MINE

"I gotta go."

"I know," Paris said with a light smile.

"The game starts at six," she said as she let him out.

Thank you, he mouthed before answering his phone and heading back to his truck.

"What's up Ma?"

"Chicken or fish…"

"Shit you decide. I'll be there in a bit."

"Okay love you…"

"Love you too."

When Bleek closed the car door behind him Sha sat up in his seat. He wiped the drool from the side of his mouth.

"How did it go?"

"Bro he is so fucking perfect. He's me in every fucking way. I was so muthafucking nervous walking in there and he just took a nigga in. He took this flawed nigga in like my absence his whole life meant nothing."

Bleek pulled away from the curb and headed to his estate. He told Sha all about the visit as they rode.

"In the morning I gotta take my boy shopping before his big game. It starts at six by the way."

"You still want me to come?" Sha asked.

"Hell yeah."

"Aight bet. I'm coming shopping in the morning too?"

"Na... ima save that time for me and him."

"When you gone tell sis?"

With the car stopped at a red light Bleek chewed on his bottom lip while he sat in thought.

"Not tonight. I can't miss that game tomorrow. Tomorrow night I'll tell her."

"Or... or you can tell her after Christmas so that way dinner is already made, we already fed, kids done opened their presents and shit."

"Na I gotta tell her before then bro because if I could have my boy under my roof for the holidays then ima try."

Bleek sighed because he knew that his ass was gonna be the one kicked out of his own house when he came clean.

"Whatever floats your boat."

Sha took his phone out and then started looking up restaurants that would be open on Christmas Day.

"Chinese food on Christmas Day is a vibe right?"

Bleek started laughing as he waited for the gate to his estate to open.

Chapter 4

"Daddy if there's a Santa then why the presents up under the tree and it's not Christmas yet?"

Bleek stopped brushing his hair in the mirror and looked behind him in Eternity's direction. Their daughter stood in the doorway of the bathroom turning her attention from her mom and dad. Bleek told Eternity that if she was still trying to push the *there's Santa* narrative that she couldn't place the presents under the tree just yet.

"Maliah, Santa can come more than once. Maybe just maybe he waits until the night before Christmas to bring your favorite thing."

"Hmmm," the young girl scratched her head causing her curly locs to bounce around, "so my Mac book pro isn't down there yet? Got it." Bleek shook his head and laughed.

"I guess not then, huh?" He said as he turned in the mirror to brush his hair some more.

"You better cut all this Santa ain't real stuff out before your sister hears it," Eternity said as she lay in the bed flipping through the channels.

"She's the one that told me he wasn't real. She said one night after bedtime she was coming to get in bed with y'all and saw you on the floor with wrapping paper and you kept saying *shit where's the scissors*."

"Maliah watch your mouth."

"Sorry Daddy, that's what Mommy said."

"Well, you tell your nosey ass sister when she gets up that all parents have to be Santa's helpers that's how he moves so fast. He drops the presents off and then the parents wrap them up," Eternity said as she sat up in the bed.

The young girl's bushy eyebrows dented as she took all of the information in.

"I mean I guess."

"If you're hungry head downstairs I'll be down in a moment to make us some breakfast. I just need to talk to Daddy real quick."

"Okay, Mommy."

The nine-year-old little chocolate beauty skipped out of the room in her grinch pajamas.

Once the girl was out of the room with the door closed behind her Bleek stood in the doorway of the bathroom and just looked at his wife. She was perfection in his eyes. The duvet covered her body but still, he saw the outlining of her curvy frame. She looked him up and down for a moment before she parted her lips.

"You got in late last night."

"I did."

Sometimes less and more and Bleek had to learn that over the years.

"And now you're leaving out early."

"I am."

41

"You wanna tell me what's this about?"

"Not yet..."

Eternity raised her eyebrow with much attitude.

"Mmm..." she hummed before sucking her teeth, "so now we're keeping secrets."

"Ma, no," he closed the space between them and sat at the foot of the bed. Never would he have ever sat with his outside clothes but he had to get his point across and fast all without disclosing too much just yet., "if I knew exactly how to tell you this then I would."

In an instant, a glossy coat covered her brown orbs.

"Is it another woman?" her voice cracked.

"Hell no, Eternity there can never be another woman. Another bitch can't hold a candle to you on your worst fucking day. Do you hear me?"

He saw the doubt written all over her face. It was the lines on her forehead from her sad expression. It was the way she chewed on her bottom lip. It was the way her nose flared as she tried to hold back the tears. She had this gut feeling for days and now it was hitting its boiling point.

"Nobody got it but you..."

The pad of his thumb wiped away the single tear that fell.

"Then what..." her tone was pleading with him.

It had taken them years to build and form the comfort that they now lived in. The comfortably that their relationship now basked and thrived in. The secret was killing her.

"Can I please just tell you tonight? Please Ma," he looked at the Richard Millie that graced his wrist, "I gotta go."

"Okay..."

He ensured her that it wasn't another woman so she took comfort in that. He kissed her button nose. I'll be back around 8:30.

"Okay..."

He grabbed her neck gently as he kissed her. He broke their lip lock to gently tap her lips once more.

"I love you. 8:30."

"8:30," she said just before he got up and rushed out of the door.

She rushed to the window and watched as he got into his truck, "I love you too," she whispered.

***

Paris swung her door open with much force. Her off days were for sleeping in and everyone knew that.

"Wha—" she stopped herself when she saw Bleek standing on the other side of the door, "good morning," she said as she wiped the side of her mouth. He stood on the other side of her door in his signature uniform, a sweatsuit. Briefly, she looked down at his print and remembered all of the fun times they had when he used to swing that lumber her way.

"It's early Malik," she said as she opened the door to let him in.

"I know I told him I would take him shopping today I want to get out before everyone else does."

"He's still sleeping..."

"Can I wake him?"

Paris held her hand out towards the stairs.

"My old office is his bedroom."

The name MJ was written on the closed room door.

When he opened the door he saw that the room was decorated with everything Minecraft. He stood up against the side of the doorway and watched for a moment as the boy slept. His chocolate foot dangled off the side of the bed while one of his arms did as well. He slept with his mouth wide open just like Maliah slept. The durag Bleek told him to put on his head the night before was damn near off. On a shelf above a computer desk, Bleek saw awards. Academic awards, sports awards the boy was indeed talented. In his absence he had mastered so much:

"Mali—"

"Shh..."

Bleek silenced her, he wanted to wake his boy up. He took off his jacket and then hung it over the back of the computer chair before slowly walking toward the side of the bed. Gently he rubbed the boy's back.

"Hey man, get up let's get you some new drip."

"Ughhh," the boy groaned.

"MJ.. come on now."

Bleek patted the boy's back twice.

"I'm up," he did a stretch before sitting up.

"Good morning Dad, morning Ma," he tossed the blanket off of his frame and then started to walk out of the room to head towards the bathroom. Paris lightly rubbed the top of his head as he passed.

"He gone be your height soon," Bleek said as he stood to his feet.

"Yeah, he reminds me every chance he gets."

Silence fell between the two.

"How is this going to work Malik?"

"I'll figure it out."

"Does your family know?" She nodded towards his hand.

He had this habit of playing with his wedding band when in her presence. A reminder of what all he could lose if a wrong move was made.

"By tonight they will."

"My teeth are brushed, face washed where to Dad?"

"Wherever you wanna go little man."

"The mall cool?" MJ asked.

"Whatever you want."

Paris walked over to MJ's closet and tossed some clothes on his bed that he could wear. A gray Nike tech sweatsuit that matched Bleek's was a perfect choice.

"I'll be waiting downstairs..."

Bleek grabbed his jacket off of the computer chair and then made his way downstairs.

As he walked down the stairs he noticed the pictures along the way. Baby pictures of MJ that looked just like his first son. Damn his genes were strong, his daughters mirrored him as well. Some would say that he put in work on the nights that his children were conceived. He stood in the foyer of Paris' home in his feelings. He handled his girls with kiddy gloves but having a son felt different. He couldn't explain the feeling but he knew that he couldn't parent them the same. Love them the same yes, but their upbringings had to be different.

"I'm ready..."

Bleek broke from his train of thought once MJ was pulling him out of the door.

"What time are you bringing him back?"

Bleek rattled off his number and told Paris to text him. He knew that MJ's game started at six so he wanted him home way before then to prepare but he didn't want to rush their day out either.

"I'm texting you now..." she called out as the pair got into the truck.

"He doesn't sit in the front he's not old enough."

"He good P, go back inside."

"Yeah Ma, you heard Dad I'm good. He letting me sit in the front how Pop Pop does." Paris didn't want to spoil her son's excitement so she kept her mouth close. She stood on her doormat as she watched Bleek back out of the driveway and then speed down the block.

***

"Dad I wanna wear those for my game tonight."

MJ pointed to a pair of sneakers that were on the wall of Footlocker.

"Okay take ya sneaker off let me see what size you wear."

MJ sat on the nearby bench and handed Bleek one sneaker from his feet. After waving over a sales associate Bleek told the man what size he needed in the sneaker that MJ had requested. Pick out six more. Any pair you want.

"Any pair?"

"Yeah boy any pair."

47

MJ stood up from the bench and then started to scan the wall. Bleek turned around and as soon as he did his eyes saw Sha and Tori walking past the Footlocker and into the Pandora store that was just across on the other side.

"Shit," he mumbled lowly as he dug into his pocket for his phone.

He listened as the phone rang three times in his ear.

"What's up boy?"

"Keep Tori in the store for a little bit..." Bleek could see Sha looking around as he held the phone close to his ear.

"I'm across from y'all in the Footlocker with MJ."

"Damn bruh, aight."

"What y'all doing in the damn mall anyway?"

"I forgot to tell Tori that my sister is in town so she said we had to get her something. I'm paying the damn girl's college fees and rent she doesn't need a damn thing from me for Christmas."

"Dad I picked what I wanted."
Bleek took his ear away from the phone.

"Aight man here I come."

"Tori go over there and pick out some more charms for your chain, get a few for Eternity too."

Bleek watched as Tori walked to what seemed to be the back of the Pandora store.

"Thanks, bro," he said into the phone.

"Mmhmm," Sha responded before hanging up.

Bleek rushed to the counter to pay for the sneakers. He carried all of the bags while he and MJ made their way to the parking garage. This was their third trip back to the car. The boy had a new wardrobe, new games, and even some earrings with a chain.

"Ya grades good right?"

"Yeah... they gotta be Ma don't play that. She wants me to be a lawyer like her and Pop Pop but I wanna play ball or build cars for real." Bleek smiled. Taking apart cars and putting them back together was his safe haven, that and the gun range.

"Playing ball is cool but having mechanics as a backup is better, aight?"

"Aight..."

Every once in a while Bleek looked over and stared at his product. MJ's head was so engaged in his phone that he didn't even notice that Bleek was looking at him.

"You hungry?" Bleek asked when they started to pass a strip of restaurants,

"Yeah."

"Wendy's cool with you?"

"Yeah fo fo fo good..."

"A what?"

His son's Floridian accent was the funniest shit to Bleek.

"A fo fo fo Dad, with the burger, nugget, fry, and a drink."

"A four for $4?"

"Yeah, that."

"You want like a toy or something?"

"Na that's for babies."

"Ya sister always want a toy..." Bleek let slip out.

Bleek ordered their food and then went around to the next window to pay.

"I have a sister?"

When Bleek turned to look at MJ his phone was in his lap and he was staring into his eyes.

"You have two."

"Here you go, sir."

The woman passed Bleek his order and he handed it to MJ.

"So like I'm a little brother?"

"Na you the big dog champ. You're older than your sisters."

"Wow..." MJ took a fry out of the bag and then ate it, "is that why you weren't with me? Because you were with my sisters."

Bleek pulled into a parking spot in Wendy's parking garage.

"Na kid, I wasn't with you because I didn't know. That's not your mom's fault either so don't give her a hard time about it. Now that I do know about you I'm not missing anything you hear me?"

"I hear you."

"We good?"

"We good..."

MJ put his balled fist out and Bleek gave him dap.

"You ready for your game later?"

"Yup," MJ picked up the small iced-out basketball pendant on his chest courtesy of his father and kissed it, "ima kill 'em Dad."

Bleek smiled with pride as he made his way back to Paris' house.

Chapter 5

The school's gymnasium was packed.

"You cut it real close earlier today," Sha whispered into Bleek's ear as they stood on the sidelines watching the two teams get ready to start the game.

"I know once I get inside I'm coming clean."

Sha placed his hand on Bleek's shoulder.

"God rest your soul."

"Shut the fuck up nigga they starting." Bleek watched with a huge grin on his face as his boy took control of the court.

In the middle of the game, Bleek looked across the court and saw that Paris was standing and clapping. When they made eye contact she waved in his direction. He gave her a head nod. Winning the game is what everyone had anticipated.

"118 to 113 how you feel my boy!?" Bleek had MJ up on his neck as everyone made it to the parking lot.

"I feel good! I knew I was gonna win though. I did what I was supposed to do. Ma are you proud?"

"Of course, I am Stinky—"

"Maaaaa..."

"Yeah my boy you did good," Paris put on a deep voice and did a little thug walk that had MJ laughing.

"You can hoop for real lil nigga."
MJ looked at Sha with uncertain eyes.

"Dad who is this?"

"That's your uncle Sha."

"I have an ant I ain't ever have an uncle before. Sup?" MJ said excitedly.

"Ain't shit, how you?" Sha responded nonchalantly.

"Ummm your language..." Paris said as she watched the encounter between her son and Sha.

"You gonna have to get used to this," Bleek said with a laugh as he put MJ down from his neck.

After the boy's feet were planted safely on the ground, Bleek stretched to give his back some relief from carrying the boy across the parking lot.

"Every time I win a game me and Ma go for pizza at the pizzeria by our house. Dad and Uncle Sha, y'all want to come?"
Bleek checked the watch on his wrist and when he noticed MJ's bushy eyebrows dip in anger he quickly responded.

"Yeah, we can go for a slice real quick. After that, I gotta head home MJ. I have to tell your sisters and stepmother about you."

"Stepmother?" The boy questioned.
Paris crouched down so that she could be eye-to-eye with her son.

53

"Yes Stink your dad has a wife and other children. I'm sure your sisters will be excited to meet you. And a stepmother is like a regular mommy but they just step in when your real mommy isn't around. I'm sure she's nice and will be excited to meet you too."

Both Sha and Bleek looked on as Paris parented. He felt blessed, other women in this situation would have drug Bleek through the mud but not Paris. She understood that Bleek had his own family and it was with the love of his life. Even when they were together she knew that there wasn't space for her when it came to how he loved. His heart was iced up and she never got the full story as to why. So she danced around the outskirts of his heart with a hand-held torch hoping to get through the icy layers to be loved by him.

When you co-parent and those relationship feelings are still involved that's when things get messy. Bleek and Paris were already headed down the right path because the relationship part of them had subsided years ago. Bleek snapped from his thoughts of how the night of coming clean would go for him when he heard MJ's little voice.

"Okay so like a bonus mommy?"

"Exactly like a bonus mommy," Paris kissed his nose and then wiped the maroon-colored lipstick off it.

"So Dad y'all coming?"

Bleek looked at Sha and waited to see what his thoughts on it were.

"We might as well enjoy the pizza... since it's gonna be the only shit we eating anyway," he said the last part in more of a whisper that only Bleek could hear. Bleek laughed at Sha before responding.

"Yeah, we coming. You riding out with me or what?"

"Actually...." MJ put his thumb and pointer finger on his chin and stood there for a while why he thought about it, "I'm gonna ride out with Ma, follow us Dad."

MJ started to walk to the back seat of Paris' car.

"You can sit in the front kiddo," Paris said as she unlocked the doors on her key fob.

"For real?"

MJ turned around with a smile so bright before rushing to the passenger side and then hopping in.

"Ima be right behind y'all. Drive safe, P one of my prized possessions is in that mufucka."

"Boy bye don't nobody drive more recklessly than you."

Paris walked to the driver's side of the car, got in, and then started the engine.

After Bleek and Sha climbed into his truck he started it and then rolled down his window. MJ rolled down the window on his side and smiled at his dad.

55

"Lead the way," Bleek said to Paris. She backed out of her parking spot and then exited the lot with Bleek following behind.

"Ty coming out here for Christmas?" Sha asked as he rolled the blunt he had been craving the whole basketball game.

"Na he didn't feel like getting all the kids together."

"That nigga got a little army going over there for sure."

"A starting five most definitely," Bleek added on.

"That nigga got the starting five and the rest of the team on the bench."
Sha and Bleek laughed at the gangsta-turned-family man that they were close to.

Right before his eyes, Bleek looked at a vehicle turnover in front of traffic in front of Paris' car.

"Why the fuck her car not stopping fast enou—"
Before he could finish his sentence, Paris' Lexus collided with the side of the minivan. Bleek stomped on his brakes so that he didn't join the accident in front of him. His heart fell in his stomach when he saw the smoke coming from the hood of Paris' car. Both Bleek and Sha swung their car door open and started to run to the car wreck up ahead.

"MJ! Paris!" Bleek screamed as the sole of his sneakers met with the pavement.

***

5 minutes earlier...

"Ma you really cool for letting me sit in the front?" MJ was geeked.

He relaxed back on the peanut butter color seats as his mom maneuvered on the streets.

"You a big boy and if your dad and pop pop allows it I guess I can bend a little."

"You dusting him Ma."

MJ looked back to see that the truck was a little further back from them when he turned around his eyes expanded in size.

"Ma!" He yelled as the car slid into the side of the minivan head-on.

The impact of the airbag hit both MJ and Paris directly in the face.

"Ah!" He screamed and couldn't stop screaming or crying. The smell of the airbags filled his nostrils.

"Ma!" He looked over to see Paris slumped into the exploded airbag and busted steering wheel.

"Ma!" The taste of pennies filled the inside of his mouth but he didn't care. His main concern was his mother.

"MJ! Paris!"

"Dad!" MJ yelled when he heard his father's voice getting closer to the car.

"Ma!"

Paris still gave no response. Bleek went to pull MJ's door open but because of the damage to the front of the car, he couldn't get it open. He looked at the minivan and instantly rage filled him.

Looking through the back window of the van he and the driver of the vehicle made eye contact. The white man's pupils doubled in size when he saw Bleek begin to walk his way. Fearing what would become of him he quickly drove off. Sirens being heard in the distance stopped Bleek from pulling his 40 glock from his waistband and dumping at the moving minivan.

"Bro leave that for another day," Sha said as he pulled open Paris' side of the door.

Bleek squinted his eyes so that he could read the plate on the minivan. With the memory of an elephant, he remembered it by heart. It was written in his mind until he delivered revenge.

"Ma!"

Bleek broke from his deadly thoughts and ran to Paris' side of the car when he heard MJ scream.

Unconscious still, Paris lay unresponsive over the steering wheel.

"Sir let us in so we can help her."

Two paramedics were on the scene along with the fire department in the police. While the paramedics were working on Paris Bleek was begging the fire department to be careful with getting his son out of the car.

***

The smell of hospitals used to be the norm for Bleek. It didn't matter what hospital in the world you were in they all smelled the same. MJ sat on the hospital bed while the doctor applied stitches to the laceration on his forehead. Bleek stared at the Minecraft backpack that he had pulled from the crushed vehicle. Leon Shaw rushed behind the hospital curtain with his wife trailing behind him. When his eyes met with Bleek's his facial expression went stone cold.

He was there for his daughter when she had gone through her pregnancy alone.

"Pop Pop!" MJ screamed out as soon as he saw his grandfather.

"Aye man wasshannn with ya huh? You in here being a big boy?"

"Yeah, I am this lady said once my stitches fall out ima look the same as before."

"That's right, baybay sit here with MJ," he said to his wife.

"Hi, Nana."

"Hi baby," she sat beside him.

"Malik a word..."

Leon nodded his head to the hallway and then began to exit. Bleek followed him out. The

59

sliding door wasn't closed good before Leon tore into the man in front of him.

"Now I don't know what kind of hocus pocus bullshit you on but—"
Bleek understood Leon's frustration but he wasn't about to take disrespect from anyone.

"I don't know what you were told but I didn't know about MJ. Now I do and I'm here one hundred percent. I'm not one of those dead beat-ass fathers. I take care of my family. That's it."

"Fuck what you do for yours that boy and his mama are mine. They are all mi—"
Leon stopped mid-conversation when he saw a group of doctors running to a room.

"That's Paris' room!"
Bleek yelled before he took off running and Leon followed behind him. By the time they both made it to the doorway everyone in the room was still.

"Time of death time of death... twenty-thirty."

Bleek caught Leon as his knees went weak beneath him.

"My baby!"
Not having anyone else to hold on to Leon held Bleek and cried on his shoulder like a baby. The doctors and Bleek let Leon have his moment. When his tears had finally subsided he knew that he had to be strong. He had to inform his wife and for that, he needed to be the support that she needed. When Bleek and Leon got back into

the room both MJ and his grandmother broke down in tears. MJ understood death because his mother had that talk with him when she thought that Bleek was dead but still, hearing about his own mother did something to him.

Bleek knew it wasn't the time to be checking his watch but he knew that he had to make it home soon.

"Leon?"

He looked up from consoling his wife when Bleek called him.

"Please let me know about funeral arrangements I will pay for whatever. I have to go."

"Dad I want to come with you!"

MJ jumped up from the hospital bed and started to race towards his father until Leon held his arm out.

"Leon let him go. It's his damn father. He's a boy and his father should raise him, it's what Paris would have wanted."

Kim, Leon's wife said before continuing to cry on his chest.

"You make sure you call me on the video when you get there okay?"

"Okay Pop Pop. I love y'all."

"We love you, baby," Kim said with watery eyes.

"Malik?"

"Sir?"

"She wanted to be cremated so we will do that. When things get situated we'll figure out together what to do with MJ's stuff at the house."

"Okay, that's cool."

Bleek looked at the grieving couple and felt for them. He wondered if that's how he and Eternity had looked when they had lost their child.

"Let's go home MJ," Bleek held his hand out and his son took it.

When Bleek made it to the lobby Sha got up from one of the chairs and followed him and MJ out.

Chapter 6

Eternity let the 90's R&B music fill the kitchen as she placed pepperonis on the homemade pizza. With the holiday just two days away she had no want to slave over a hot stove the days leading up to Christmas. She looked at the time on the stainless steel microwave and then sighed when 9pm was lit in the neon green color. *He said he would be back at 8:30.* She thought to herself. Malik was prompt, and always on time because he valued his own time so he didn't play with others.

"Mommy is the pizza ready yet? I'm tired of pretending to eat Maylee's fake donuts. I'm hungry in real life."

Eternity turned around to see her nine-year-old standing in the doorway of the kitchen with one hand on her stomach and the other on her hip. Sassy. She was the spitting image of Malik with the attitude of Eternity.

"Here sissyyyy have more donut," Maylee came running full speed into the kitchen with a play plate in her hand. On the plate was a fake chocolate donut with sprinkles.

"Seeeee," Maliah rolled her eyes as she held her small hand out to show her mother what she meant.

"What sissy it's good! Mommy have some."

Maylee's tight curls bounced as she skipped over to her mother.

Eternity quickly put the pizza into the oven before grabbing the plate from Maylee.

"Yummmm," she pretended to take a bite.

Maylee smiled brightly showing the two missing front teeth.

"Seeeee sissy yummy mommy said yummm."

Please deactivate alarm now

"Daddy!"

"Daddy!"

Both girls took off running towards the front door. Whenever he left the girls inside by themselves the alarm system being on was a must. Not only was the alarm tied to law enforcement but also a team of Florida's finest gangsters would be there in less than five minutes.

Please deactivate alarm now

The alarm sounded again.

"Girls!" Eternity called out as she quickly walked towards the front door. Malik would never let the alarm alert go off twice.

"Girls..." Eternity rounded the wall that led to the foyer.

"Who that?" Maliah started at her dad and uncle that stood in the doorway with the unknown guest.

Eternity stood behind her girls with eyeballs that began to water. The small child standing directly next to Malik looked so broken. Stitches were on a cut on his forehead that was obviously fresh because there was blood at the top of the cream Polo zip-up hoodie he wore. Eternity bit her bottom lip as her nostrils flared, she was trying to keep her tears down. Sha deactivated the alarm so that it didn't sound again.

He sighed because he always had a front town seat to the awkward, uncomfortable stages of the love story called Eternity and Bleek. Eternity breathed heavily as she took in the image in front of her. The boy beside her husband was a spitting view of him, he favored her children as well. The only difference was his skin was a shade darker than her husband's and her children's.

"Daddy…. Who that?"
Before anyone else could speak Eternity turned around and then walked back towards the kitchen.

"Y'all go in the living room with uncle Sha. I need to ima— Eternity…" he called out.
When he stepped forward MJ grabbed his arm.

"Aye little man chill out with me he gone be back," Sha tossed his arm over the young boy and then led the way to the living room, "let's go, little divas, I'll let y'all turn on that frozen shit."

Bleek heard the sound of footsteps racing toward the living room as he followed behind his wife. Bleek stood in the kitchen's opening and watched as Eternity pulled the pizza from the oven.

Get on my knees for you
Ooh, baby
What else is there to do?
I don't know, I don't know, but I'll cry

Lady, I will cry for you tonight, tonight (yeah)

Bleek listened to Jodeci as he watched her open one of the drawers and pull the pizza cutter from it.

"Is this what you had to tell me? You have a son?"
She never turned around to face him.

He always demanded eye contact when they spoke but he was grateful that she hadn't turned around because tears had begun to fall from his eyes. He thought about how far they had come. He thought about the son that they had lost that would have been the same age as MJ.

It's amazing what you do
To keep me falling in love with you

Girl, you all that I know
Where else can I go?

"Well don't even answer that," she tossed the cutter into the sink after cutting slices. After opening the oak-colored upper cabinets she pulled three plates down, "how old is he?" Bleek used the back of his hand to wipe his face clean.

"I never cheated on you, Ma."

She blew out a sharp breath but didn't offer a response. He knew her well enough to know that he had another hot second to respond before one of the square plates would come hurling at his head.

"He's ten."

"What happened tonight?"

She put one slice of pizza on each plate and then turned around to face her husband. She looked at the blood that covered his jacket too. While the pizza cooled he explained everything to her. How he discovered that he was MJ's father, the initial meet, the shopping spree, the basketball game, and then the car accident. He explained Paris' death and how he had to issue revenge on the hit-and-run driver.

"You need to remember that one day that boy will follow your example, not your advice. Your killer days ended with the birth of the girls. Don't resort back to that. Whoever that driver is God will deliver a worse punishment."

Bleek nodded as he listened to Eternity.

"He looks just fucking like you, he looks like them," she added as she blew out a sharp breath.

He strolled in her direction, slowly, unsure of how she would react to him being so close to her. His eyes scanned the counter behind her searching for knives. He saw the set in the butcher block behind her. He tried to read her body language.

"I'm sorry," he was taking ownership of the situation, "I know this is a lot, and if you want to leave Ma I just... I need you and my girls," his eyes began to water again, "I need my girls, all of y'all. I just can't... he's—"

"He's your son, he's family, he's *our* family."

Bleek grabbed Eternity by the chin and then kissed her deeply. When he felt her bottom lip quiver he opened his eyes to see that tears were streaming down her pudgy cheeks.

"Ma look at me."

Her eyes were closed tightly. Their baby's face flashed in her mind. His pudgy chocolate face. She remembered how his dimples deepened with the gummy grin he would do when she would kiss all over his neck.

"Ma..."

She shot her eyes open and then gazed into his brown eyes.

"I love you."

"I know," and she did.

His eyes squinted. They had the phase of her professing her love and he never did the same because she never knew what she wanted. The *I know* was his line and here she was using it.

"I love you..."

He kissed her button nose.

"I love you..." she said again.

He kissed her lips. She blew out a quick breath to stop the tears on the horizon. He used his pointer and thumb to pick up the piece to her chain.

Baby feet in white gold was a locket with a piece of their son's umbilical cord inside. He kissed the piece before kissing her lips again.

"Grab those two plates," she said as she grabbed the last one.

She led the way into the living room.

"No I don't want any more fake donuts," MJ said as he crossed his arms across his chest.

"Fine," Maylee snatched the plate, "uncle Sha say ahhh"

"Hell na I don't want that shit either." Eternity had to laugh as she walked in on the encounter between the kids and Sha.

"Here's the pizza y'all come sit at y'all table. MJ..."

Brown round eyes looked up at Eternity. After placing the plate in her hand down on the table she bent down next to one of the empty chairs at the table.

"Come," he stood and then played with the bottom of his shirt.

It was obvious that the boy was nervous. His eyes rolled over in Bleek's direction. He stood on watching the encounter between his wife and his son. Eternity noticed the Minecraft socks he had on his feet. He was the cutest thing to her, he was the smallest version of Bleek.

"My name is Eternity, I'm their mom. Your dad told me that your mom is in heaven. Do you mind me being your stepmom?"

His little eyes watered.

"Dad said my mom is with me forever. Your name is Eternity that means forever. Will you be with me forever too?"

"Aww," Eternity's eyes watered, "can I hug you?"

She opened her arms. She wasn't sure if he would be closed off but once she felt his little frame in her arms she hugged him tightly.

"Yes, I'm here forever okay. Let's get you changed out of these bloody clothes so you can have some pizza okay? Babe?"

Eternity turned around and saw Bleek was eyes on them.

"Does he have anything to change into for the night?"

"I have my ball shorts that I wore for my game."

Eternity turned back to MJ.

"Congrats on your win."

70

MJ smiled and then hugged Eternity again.

"Having a bonus mommy is gonna be fun. Dad the bag is in your truck."

Bleek started to walk towards the front door to get the bag out of the car.

"Wait up Dad, let me come with you."

Eternity watched as the two made their exit.

"Welp..." Sha stood from the sofa and then did a light stretch, "so we're good on Christmas food right? Everything cool?"

Eternity walked over to the sofa and then picked up one of the pillows from it. She tossed it at Sha, "boy get the fuck out of my house," she laughed.

"No really sis you good?"

Eternity took a deep breath and then smiled.

"Yeah..."

"You not but you trying like a muthafucka and that's all that matters."

He walked over and then gave her a hug before mushing her away from him. He was affectionate but only when he wanted to be.

"Oh yeah, heads up. Tori's ass gonna be calling you because I gotta explain why the fuck I ain't been answering her calls since earlier today."

Bleek and MJ walked back into the house as Sha was walking out.

"I'll see y'all on Christmas."

"Dad, can I call my Pop Pop? I told him that I would call when we got here."

"Yeah give him a call while you change. Here take your backpack and switch ya clothes out real quick okay? The bathroom is right there," Bleek pointed to the door down the hall and on the left."

"Aight," MJ took the bag from him and then headed in the direction of the bathroom.

"Can I have more?" Maylee asked as she chewed on the crust of the pizza.
Eternity picked up the two empty plates and then started to walk toward the kitchen.

"Mommy that boy is calling Daddy... Dad. Why?"

Bleek was waiting on one of the girls to ask what was going on. Both girls were outspoken but Bleek knew that Maliah would be the first one to say something. He crouched down at their table.

"Well... that boy's name is MJ and he is y'all big brother."
Maylee opened her mouth animatedly. She turned to Maliah and then stuck her tongue out.

"Ahh haa sissy you no boss me around no more. You a little sister too."
Maliah turned in Maylee's direction and then rolled her eyes.

"What you think about that Maliah?" Bleek was reading his daughter and it was evident that she had an attitude.

"I think... I think he has to protect us because you said boys are supposed to protect girls right?"

"Yeah, that's right mama."

Eternity smiled and then went into the kitchen to get the extra pizza slice for Maylee. As she walked back into the living room, MJ was walking back into the living room as well.

"Brothaaaaa," Maylee sang as soon as MJ entered the room.

He smiled at Maylee and then took the seat next to her in front of the plate that had a slice on it. He began to eat his food.

"Mommy, I'm sleepy can I go to bed?" Maliah asked as she wiped her mouth and hands with the paper towel that was on the table.

Eternity knew her daughter and could tell that she was bothered by the extra presence.

"Yeah boo go ahead to your room. I'll be up in a bit okay?"

"Okay, goodnight..."

Bleek held his arms open for the hug that she had always given him before bed but when she stood from the table and then made her exit he dropped his arms at his sides.

Eternity looked at Bleek and saw the defeat spread across his face. Maliah was his entire world. From the day that she was born, she had stolen a whole different side of his heart that Eternity didn't even have access to.

"Set MJ up in one of the spare bedrooms. Tomorrow we will have his room set up," Eternity looked in MJ's direction, "how does your own room sound big man?"

MJ chewed on his pizza and then stuck his thumbs up in approval.

"I'll go handle her."

Bleek grabbed her arm and then pulled her into his embrace. He gently tapped her lips and that's only because the children were watching. She kissed him back and then walked away from him. He held onto her hand until the space in between them caused their fingers to stop touching.

"You can stay in the spare bedroom with him tonight, I know he is going to need you close."

Bleek shook his head up and down as he watched her walk away and then climb the stairs. He stared in her direction until he couldn't see her anymore. She was the shit. A damn good woman, a strong ass woman, and he was honored and blessed to call her his.

Chapter 7

Eternity slowly walked into Maliah's room and saw that she was back-propped against the headboard with her arms folded across her chest.

"You get a sixty-second window go." Eternity said as she sat at the foot of the full-sized bed. She was big on giving her children freedom of speech and with window periods they could say whatever was on their minds. She remembered when she first introduced Maliah to the *open window* the girl sat there for sixty full seconds saying every curse word in the book. Her daughter stared into her eyes.

"Use your time wisely."

"I don't want Daddy to love me less because he has another kid. He can do boy stuff with MJ and they can have their own special time and I don't like that because he's my daddy and I'm supposed to only have special time with him. I already have to share him with Maylee."

"Daddy won't love you any less just because he has another kid baby girl. You see how he can love you and your sister equally?" Eternity placed the hair in front of Maliah's face behind her ear. She shook her tiny head up and down.

"Right so Daddy can love all of us equally. I have to learn to love MJ and so do you and your sister. You should be happy this means we have more family. And guess what?"

"What?"

Eternity moved closer to Maliah before she whispered, "I think Daddy needed a boy around. It may give him a little fighting chance when we vote on things."

Maliah smiled because that meant that they wouldn't be tied anymore they had one extra person to break the tie.

"Plus," Eternity started to tickle Maliah, "you get to be a spoiled little sister and you don't have to worry about being the older sibling anymore."

"Mommy stopppp," Maliah laughed as she tried to cover herself with the blanket to stop Eternity's tickle attack.

"Do you feel better now?" Eternity asked as she stopped tickling her child.

"Yes!"

"Okay let me tuck you in."

Maliah got comfortable in the bed and then waited for Eternity to toss the blanket in the air and let it fall down on her small frame as she always did. Maliah moved her feet around the sheets quickly as the comforter slowly landed over her.

"Night sissyyyy! Night Mommy!" Maylee yelled as she, Bleek, and MJ was walking past the room.

"Goodnight sissy... Goodnight brother," Maliah said in response.

MJ walked back and stood in the doorway.

"Goodnight sis," he said before he quickly jogged to catch up with Bleek and Maylee. Eternity yawned before kissing Maliah on the forehead.

"You get in bed Mommy, you're sleepy too."

"Goodnight baby."

"Goodnight Mommy."

Eternity turned off Maliah's room light and when she did the LED lights behind her headboard lit up pink.

Eternity dragged her feet across the carpet as she made her way to her and Bleek's room. The day was a long one and she needed to mentally unwind. She walked into the bathroom connected to their room and then ran her bathwater and added her oils and soaps. The jetted tub stood in the middle of the floor. She came out of her clothes and then lit two candles before connecting her phone to the speaker. She saw that Tori had called her three times. She put her phone on do not disturb before pressing shuffle on a music playlist she named *Just breathe...*

A small group of songs that she played on repeat when her mind was troubled. She turned off the water because the bubbles were at the perfect level. She undressed as the music played loudly.

Hey, should I pray? Should I pray, yeah
To myself? To a God?
To a savior who can

Unbreak the broken

She slowly placed her foot into the tub. She stood in the tub just looking at her reflection in the mirror. The stretch marks that extended across her abdomen were a clear indication that she had given birth. With each stretchmark, she knew which pregnancy it had come from. The bottom half of her stomach was Maylee's area, the middle and sides were all Maliah now that top part was her baby boy. Her eyes watered as she held onto her stomach. She eased her body into the hot water and then laid back in the tub.

"Hey, Siri…"

"Hmmm?"

"Play this song on repeat."

The melody was speaking to her. She wanted the moment to sulk and James Arthur was allowing her to do just that. She laid her head back on the cushion that was inside the back area of the tub. *Breathe…* she was coaching herself because Bleek wasn't there to do it. She knew that his boy needed him. The child had lost his mom and she would never imagine she knew what that felt like. But Bleek did, he knew what it was like to see a motherly figure die right in front of you. He could relate where she couldn't.

78

As she closed her eyes and saw the young boy's face that was now a new resident in her home her chest jolted up and down as she cried out. He looked so much like what she thought her son would grow into. She sniffled loudly and when she did she smelled his scent. Nishane, only the best because he wouldn't roll any other way. That expensive ass scent ran $600 a bottle but lasted on him all day. Her hair would smell of it every single time she lay on his chest.

Under other circumstances, her garden would have wet in pleasure off that smell alone. When she tried to quickly clean her face with her nearby rag, she felt his strong hands tap her back twice so she scooted up. When she felt his muscular frame ease into the water behind her, she waited for him to sit down before she laid back onto him. Strong dick laid on her back as he wrapped his strong arms around her body.

Underneath our bad blood
We've still got a sanctum, home
Still a home, still a home here
It's not too late to build it back

He kissed the sides of her face as she cried freely. He waited for MJ to fall asleep before he came looking for his wife. On the walk to his bedroom when he heard this song playing he knew that she was taking her mental break. So many nights this same song played on repeat

79

when she felt like she couldn't deal. Each pregnancy came with a hardship postpartum because her mind went exactly where it was right now. So, he knew exactly how to deal with the mental side of Eternity.

"Come on baby," he grabbed the rag that was draped over the side of the tub and then started to wash her.

"Pull me out...pull me out," she sang and cried. He cried right with her. He prayed, hoping that they could make it through this.

Knowing her inside and out he knew that she wouldn't break until she was in her own solitude. He washed her completely and didn't even bother to wash. This time was strictly for her. He had been neglecting her these past couple of days and that was out. After he finished washing her he dried her off and then turned the music off after blowing out the candles. Carrying her to their bed was nothing. He would bench press her weight on a light day. After laying her in the bed he lay beside her.

"Go and sleep with MJ he needs to—"

"You need me right now he's sleeping, I'll be in there by morning. Come here," he opened his arms up and she lay on his chest.

"Say it ... just say it."
He knew what she needed from him.
"*Breathe...*"
Instantly she could just a little better.

"You must think I'm that nigga Ethic or some shit."

Eternity laughed at him referring to a book bae of hers. He was the only man that could get her time beside him. When they both stopped laughing he kissed the top of her head.

"I love you," she said before snugging her head onto his chest.

Body to body they lay with nothing over them but the comforter.

"I love you more," he kissed the top of her head again before staring up at the ceiling. Blessed beyond measure he didn't know when God decided that he was the kind of man that deserved all the good shit he had been given.

"Thank you," he mouthed to the man above and he truly was indeed thankful.

Eternity began to snore lightly on his chest. After thirty minutes he eased from under her and then threw some pajamas on. He yawned as he made his way to the extra bedroom that MJ was occupying. The little boy had his arm dangled off the bed. Bleek lay beside him. Not being able to sleep, he looked around the room and made a mental note of things to get to make the room more comfortable for MJ. His blinks started to feel heavier as he began to doze off.

Chapter 8

Bleek woke to the sound of children running through the house. He sat up in the bed and saw that the space beside him was empty.

"Eternity bout to cuss they ass out." He mumbled as he exited the spare bedroom and walked to his bedroom to find that the bed was made up. He walked downstairs and saw that the kids were playing freeze tag in the living room.

"Y'all better calm down before y'all break some shit."
All of the kids stopped running and then found a spot on the couch.

"Maylee, Maliah, where's your mother?"
Maliah shrugged her shoulders, "I don't know Daddy. Mommy gave us breakfast and then she said she will be back. She said to be good and don't wake you."

"So much for the not waking me part," he huffed under his breath.
He walked to the kitchen to get his phone. The note on the refrigerator caught his attention.

Left to go and get things for MJ. Your plate is in the microwave.
- E

She drew a heart next to her name. He grabbed his phone and saw that it was dead. He put it on the charger in the kitchen before opening the microwave. Pancakes, eggs, and turkey bacon were on his plate. When he grabbed a piece of bacon he felt that it was still warm. *She must have just left.* He thought to himself as he grabbed the entire plate out of the microwave and then made his way to the living room to be with his kids.

✳✳✳

"You better get an Xbox too, *step mommy.*"

"Shut up," Eternity fussed at her sister as she pushed the cart through Walmart.

Christmas Eve and she was out with the last to last-minute shoppers. She saw this creeper plush toy from Minecraft and started pushing her cart at full speed.

"Lady give me that damn toy I know you saw me walking over here for it."

"Sis, what is happening?" Tori asked as she pushed the phone closer into her ear to hear Eternity's background.

"This bitch is trynna take this toy she saw me coming to get."

"You bitch!"
Tori heard tussling in her ear.

"Hellooooo," Tori yelled into the phone.

"Yeah bitch better gone head."

"Eternity?"

"Yeah, Tori Tee."

"The fuck just happened?"

"Had to rough this bitch up a bit for this Minecraft toy. Now… next I need to get him some pajamas."

"Girlllllll," Tori dragged, "I know you not beating people up in the Walmart. Can you say ghetto?"

"I don't care, Chaz will be at the house in a bit with his bed set and décor I want everything perfect. I want him to feel comfortable in our home. I'm going to the mall for the pickup order. I had everything pre-wrapped for him so it can just be added under the tree.

"You really dope as shit, sis."

Eternity smiled. Compliments from her baby sister always warmed her heart.

"I mean I'm trying. What time y'all coming to the house tomorrow?"

"We'll be there in the morning. Whatever time the Lord opens my eyes."

Eternity laughed before responding, "aight well let me finish these runarounds I'm sure the kids are driving Bleek crazy inside."

"Okay sis, I love you."

"I love you more."

Eternity ended the line and she waved over a Walmart employee to help her get the Minecraft game out of the showcase.

***

Bleek watched on the monitor as a work van followed by a box truck pulled up to the gates of his estate.

"Who's that Dad?"

MJ sat next to him on the sofa as they watched football highlights on ESPN. The girls were in their own little world, Maliah playing on her iPad while Maylee sat in the middle of the living room playing with her dolls. His phone rang.

"Yeah?"

"Hey hubby, I spoke to wifey this morning and we have things for little man. Let us in. In about an hour he is going to have the room of his dreams."

Bleek bit his bottom lip to keep the emotions at bay. His damn woman was the shit, his lady was making dreams come true in under twenty-four hours. All while, still feeling her own pain. He pressed three buttons on his phone and then the gates slowly started to open.

On the camera, he saw Eternity's white range rover speed in just before the gates began closing.

"Stay here lil man, watch your sisters."

"Okay," MJ placed his phone into his lap and just watched the girls play.

Bleek laughed to himself he didn't mean it literally but he could see how serious his son was taking on the role of being a big brother.

85

When he got to the front door he propped it open so that the workers can get started. Eternity hopped out of her truck and then quickly walked to the front door.

"Everything is in the trunk put those under the tree please."

He grabbed her arm as she walked past and then pulled her in close for a kiss. Their lips locked and for a moment their tongues danced to a tune that only the two of them knew. The same tune that they had been dancing with each other for over ten years.

"Ewww all that public display of affection," Chaz teased as he walked in the door behind Eternity.

"Show me which room is getting the makeover hunny."

Eternity started to walk up the stairs while Chaz followed behind her. Bleek went out to the car and then just stood and stared at all of the presents that were neatly wrapped in silver, white, and navy blue wrapping paper. It matched their Christmas tree perfectly.

The girls had tons of presents under the tree and to make sure that their new addition to the family did not feel left out Eternity spent the day before the holiday shopping for him. Bleek looked up to the heavens and thanked God. He knew that Eternity had always been a blessing in his life but now, now he knew that she was put into his life to show him that even after all of the bad shit he had done in life and had done to other people that he deserved his own happy ending.

It took him multiple trips but he was finally able to get all of the gifts inside and under the tree.

"Daddy, what is this? From the store huh?"

"No."

"Yes huh," Maylee said with attitude, "see sissy told you Santa isn't real."

"Yeah he is sis," MJ jumped down from the couch and then walked over to his littlest sister, "Santa gotta be real because for Christmas I didn't want to be the only kid anymore, and now look I got you two."
Maylee smiled and then hugged her brother. Maliah put her iPad down and then looked at her siblings.

"Yeah having a brother isn't bad. Even if that scar on your head makes you look like Harry Potter," she picked her iPad up and then finished playing her game.

MJ screwed his face up at her and then gently touched the tender scar and stitches that was on his forehead.

"In a few weeks the stitches will come out kiddo," Bleek said as he patted his back.
For hours the kids ran around and played as Bleek sat in the living room watching as people

entered and exited his home. Transforming one of the extra bedrooms into Minecraft madness was taking longer than expected but Chaz and his team were doing the damn thing.

"Well, boo thing today was a pleasure. Take a video of the reveal so that we can add it to our content," Chaz kissed both of Eternity's cheeks before waving at Bleek and then making his exit with his team following behind.

Eternity looked into Bleek's eyes and then smiled brightly. She was proud of herself for the day she had. Having MJ see his room was going to make her feel even better.

"MJ?"

"Yes?"

"Can you come upstairs with me, well can everyone come upstairs with me?"
Eternity used the back of her hand to wipe the light coat of sweat that had formed on her forehead.

"Let's go gang," Bleek led the way upstairs.
Eternity made sure to follow behind MJ. She pulled her phone from her back pocket as Bleek led the way.

"Ohhhh snap is this my room now guys?" Like the girls, MJ had his name written on his door in whatever character he liked.

Since Eternity noticed his Minecraft socks and backpack from the night before, she went Minecraft crazy. Everyone stood outside of the door that was labeled MJ, the name was written in the same TNT font that the game used. MJ turned around to face Eternity and then she nodded her head to the door to let him know that it was okay to open it. Once he opened the door he ran full speed towards the full-sized bed.

"A creeper and Iron Golem!"

"Look at this!" Maylee ran over to the bean bag chair and then jumped on it.

"This is cute," Maliah said as she walked around the room and looked at everything inside.

"Now y'all all have y'all own space. Everybody cool?"

"Yeah," everyone said in unison.

Maylee ran out of the room and then returned with some dolls.

"Mayyyyy nooo."

"Yesss brotha look," Maylee sat a baby doll on the edge of his bed.

"Yuppp Maylee bring all the dolls in here how you do my room."
MJ slapped his head in frustration.

"Mr. Browne?"

"Yes, Mrs. Browne?"

"Would you like to help me prep dinner for tomorrow?"
Bleek screwed his face up but he knew better than to decline.

"Lead the way, my love."

Eternity made her way to the kitchen with Bleek following behind. He watched as her ass jiggled with every step down a stair in her house gown.

"Mrs. Browne?"

"Yes, love?" Eternity turned around and saw that Bleek had that look.
He looked her up and down and that made her blush. She smiled hard like the eighteen-year-old girl that had just come home from juvenile detention. For hours he helped her prep the ham, the baked Mac and cheese, and the ziti, the list for the next day was long. Cooking together was a love language for them.

"It's quiet upstairs," Eternity said as she covered the last meal with aluminum foil.

"That mean gang is sleep," Bleek turned on the small monitor that was on the kitchen counter.

Every room had cameras in them. When he got to MJ's room he saw that Maylee was sleeping on the bean bag chair while Maliah was knocked out across the foot on MJ's bed. MJ was sleeping at the top of his bed.

"Yeah gang is knocked out," Bleek turned the monitor for Eternity to see before he continued, "the snow machine will be here early in the morning so they'll be able to play before dinner. Ma?"

"Yes, baby?" Eternity handed Bleek the pan and then he placed it into the fridge.

"I know we plan these Christmas pictures way in advanced with the matching pajamas but I don't want MJ to feel left out can we pass on the holiday picture this year?"

"MJ will not be left out because I got the same pajamas for him. He will be included in tradition."

Bleek walked over to her and then kissed her deeply.

"How did I get so lucky?"

"Blame it on the ghetto-ass Brooklyn shootouts."

They both laughed as they kissed repeatedly. They both thought back to how they had first met. He protected her when bullets were flying and he had been protecting her ever since. Bleek grabbed her by the hand and then lifted her arm above her head. He spun her around in a twirl before pulling her into his embrace. She felt the pistol he had on his waist and her knees almost went weak. It was that hood shit that she would forever love. They rocked from side to side to silence. Lost in their own world just enjoying the stillness of the house. Just enjoying the pureness of their love. A Merry Christmas it was because they had each other, they had THEIR kids and they had their love.

THE END

*** Don't forget to leave those reviews ***